BUBBA

Happily
Ever After

DEBORAH DOMINGUEZ, MFT
RICHARD ENGEL

ILLUSTRATED BY
SIERRA MON ANN VIDAL

To order additional copies of this book, contact:
Xlibris
1-888-795-4274
www.Xlibris.com
Orders@Xlibris.com

Illustrated by Sierra Mon Ann Vidal

ISBN: Softcover   978-1-7960-6942-6
         Hardcover   978-1-7960-6943-3
         EBook   978-1-7960-6941-9

Library of Congress Control Number: 2018901179

Print information available on the last page.

Rev. date: 10/31/2019

BUBBA

Happily Ever After

DEBORAH DOMINGUEZ, MFT
RICHARD ENGEL

ILLUSTRATED BY
SIERRA MON ANN VIDAL

CONTENTS

SUMMARY OF THE FIRST BOOK

A gerbil named Bubba loved Debi but had a strong desire to roam the world and experience adventure. He escaped his habitat and found a way to fly to Europe in a carry-on bag, to eat in a ritzy hotel, to escape near death twice (by a cat and by drowning in the Mediterranean Sea), to enjoy art at the Louvre museum, and to save a missionary project in Libya. After all that he found his love for Debi mattered more and he returned to her with the help of the missionaries. During the last two years he has enjoyed living again with Debi, but not everything is OK.

CHAPTER ONE

A Good Life Disturbed

Bubba's habitat became a place of safety, a home to rest in, and it has been for two years since saving the Libyan missionaries. Debi removed the hated yellow door so Bubba could come and go as he pleased. Dog remained in his dog run outside, and Brother stopped shaking the habitat just to tease Bubba. His life was pleasant and quiet.

Only Father worried Bubba. *After Father's visit last night I know what he wants to do,* Bubba thought to himself. *He whispered to me he's been watching me and is convinced he could make good money with me, a gerbil who can write on a laptop and think like a human. He told me he'd use me to make his life easier. He said everyone kept the secret so far but all he had to do was go to a newspaper and tell them about my gift. It would be easy, he said. He would do it soon, too. It was like a threat or something,* Bubba thought. It made Bubba very, very uncomfortable.

He looked around his home again. He had to admit something was truly nagging at him besides Father; he didn't know what it was, couldn't put his paw on it, but Bubba loved his life. He began to think, *Look at this place; it's always warm and dry (remembering the sinking boat), safer (recalling the bad guys in Libya), and Debi is so loving when she comes home from school. I even go out with her on weekends when it's safe to do so. I've seen enough of the world on my own and every mall for miles around with Debi (he chuckled to himself). I'm clean. I'm comfortable. I'm never hungry or thirsty. My habitat is beautiful. And I can come and go anytime. But I'm afraid Father is planning something for me I won't like.*

It was very early in the morning, so Bubba tried to go back to sleep, but he couldn't get the two problems off his mind. First, he was very aware he could do something no other gerbil, or animal for that matter, could do. He could read, type on a laptop, understand what people were saying to him and answer with a nod or shake of his head to answer the yes and no questions. He could even understand Father's interest in him. *But what's the reason I have this gift?*

That brought up question number two. There must be a greater reason he can do these things. *Certainly, being a famous gerbil making lots of money can't be the reason I can think and write like a human*, he thought. And Bubba tossed and turned until he decided he needed to see Debi right away.

He left his habitat and slid down to the floor. He scampered through the dark house and entered Debi's room. In a moment he was beside her head pushing his paws lightly on her cheek. He'd done this before so she awoke without surprise.

"Bubba, what do you want? It's not even light yet," she whispered. She rolled over to go back to sleep.

Bubba jumped into her hair and rolled around in it.

That woke her up. As she untangled Bubba from her hair she said, "Hang on. I'll boot my laptop. This better be good."

CHAPTER TWO

Decisions Made

Debi wasn't exactly thrilled by being awakened. It was the first time in a long time that he woke her up so early. In fact, the last time was just after he came home and he wanted to check to make sure she was "real." There also were times when he woke her just to say he loved her.

"Bubba, here," she said quietly as she laid out her laptop for him. "What's got you so excited?"

He shook his head.

"You're not excited? What do you call waking me up to talk before the sun is up?" she whispered again.

Bubba stepped onto the computer and began to type. "I couldn't sleep because of a couple of things bugging me. I finally need to talk about them."

"And this afternoon wouldn't work? OK. Do you want to make this a nod and shake session? It might be easier."

Bubba nodded and stepped off the laptop.

"Well, are you getting an urge to roam again?"

Bubba shook his head vigorously no.

"Oh, good. I thought maybe you were getting itchy to see the world." She paused. "Let's see. A couple of things are waking you up so you can't sleep. Funny, I thought little animals had no worries. Hum."

Bubba pantomimed laughing by holding his belly, making it clear he didn't think it was very funny at all. He returned to the laptop and typed, "Remember, I am a human thinker, therefore I can worry like you and Father. But to the issue, think of questions about Father and my present life. Those are the two issues."

"Well, let's see. Father likes you and…"

Bubba jumped up and down, shaking his head.

"…Bubba, do you think Father doesn't like you?"

Bubba shrugged and carefully and slowly shook his head no.

"Oh, my. That's not good. Is he bugging you or something?"

Bubba nodded vigorously and stepped onto the laptop again. He wrote, "Think TV, being a star"

"Did he say he was going to make you famous and make you a star on TV?"

Bubba shook his head and entered, "Think money."

"Did my Father say he wanted to get rich by putting you in front of the world and making lots of money off your gift?"

Bubba nodded yes sadly.

"I heard him talking about it to Mom in the kitchen. He thinks we can get free of money worries, buy a new car, and live the life of luxury. Bubba, I think he is just trying to find a way to ease things up on him and the family. My dad is a good man but has worries just like you. What you can do is very unusual. I would be remarkable to many people if we revealed it."

A long moment passed before Bubba typed, "I don't know what to say but I know being a star doesn't sound like a good life. I know I was selfish leaving the first time. It was all about me and my desire to roam. I don't want my refusal to be a sideshow to seem selfish this time either, but your father wasn't talking to me like a family member. He seemed harsh. Like the decision for him was already made. Besides, it doesn't help with the other issue. Like your dad, I feel I should be doing something. I just don't know what it is." Bubba fell off the laptop onto Debi's bedspread out of breath.

"Humm, I don't know what to do, Bubba. I think we can get help with Father's issue, but if you don't know what you should be doing how can anyone else?" She picked him and cuddled him for a few minutes. "Tell you what, after breakfast we'll go see Pastor. I bet he can help."

Bubba nodded yes, and with that they both fell back asleep.

CHAPTER THREE

A New Direction for Bubba

Bubba and Debi walked a mile-and-a-half through Moorpark to Pastor's home. It was more than pleasant with a zephyr breeze and a temperature in the mid-seventies. They walked and looked at the hillsides blossoming in golden and purple springtime flowers, and they saw occasional rabbits jumping through the sage and tall grass.

Pastor's car was in the driveway.

"What will we say, Bubba?"

Bubba shrugged. *I hope he can help*, he thought.

Pastor was surprised to see them but asked them into the living room where comfortable chairs awaited him and Debi. Pastor also went to his study and retrieved his laptop for Bubba.

"Debi, you look concerned about something. Let's pray." They all bowed their heads. "Dear Lord, I pray for Debi and Bubba now, that what concerns them might be brought to our attention clearly and fully, and we pray further for wisdom as we talk about their need. We know, Lord, that you love them and wish the best for them. Lead us to that answer, Lord. Amen

"OK. What can be on your minds? Debi, why don't you start this out."

"Well, Pastor, you know that for more than two years we've kept Bubba's human ability to use language secret. Even my brother hasn't said anything and that's amazing. The problem is Father has spoken with Bubba several times, the latest just last night, about making Bubba some kind of money-making animal to help with family finances."

"Is that correct, Bubba?"

He nodded yes emphatically.

"Go on, Debi."

"Anyway, Bubba has messaged me that my dad also inferred Bubba was called to be a star, like Bubba must do this to fulfill his place on earth or something. I can't understand why Father is thinking like that, and Bubba isn't sure what he should do," she explained.

"Well, let's run over what's gone on for the last couple of years. I've never spoken with your mom or dad about Bubba either on the street or in church, but I know Bubba's been on our minds. I've prayed numerous times about him and his ability to use a laptop but I have yet to have any feeling that we'll learn why Bubba was given this very amazing gift." After a pause Pastor turned to Bubba. "You certainly have had the same questions about yourself, right?"

Bubba nodded, then stepped onto the laptop and wrote, "I know what I have is pretty special. It's nagged at me for a while now. Father just brings it up as if there is only one career I can have with my talent. I've known since I came home that I could text a news station or newspaper and reveal what I can do, I watch television and know what's going on. I COULD be a star. I just don't feel that's the goal of this gift."

Debi jumped in. "But Bubba, my dad is probably right. There are few things you can do as an intelligent, communicating gerbil. Maybe we should just go ahead and do something like that."

"Look, guys, we have to slow it down. We asked for wisdom together for the first time just a few minutes ago. The answer won't normally come that fast. We need to consider this for a while. Obviously, we've all been thinking about this a lot. Everyone has."

Bubba and Debi nodded yes together.

"What if Bubba stays with me today while I do my pastor stuff, Debi, and I bring him home after dinner? He and I can talk this over in the time between the people we visit. And I'll talk with your dad tomorrow. If your dad asks about Bubba just tell him he's with me because he was curious about what I do…like a gerbil fieldtrip. If your dad asks, be truthful. I'm helping Bubba him with a personal struggle."

After some small talk Bubba jumped into the pastor's coat pocket and Debi headed home praying this beautiful day would bring answers for Bubba.

CHAPTER FOUR

Bubba's New Friend

Bubba was happy to be with Pastor and comfortably riding in his coat's high pocket. It brought back good memories of Libya and the exciting trip home. It also gave him a great view hanging on inside the pocket's edge. He was so far off the ground. At times like this he realized how low to the ground he was on his own legs.

Pastor already told Bubba they were going to go by church to read an essay by a theology student whose theme dealt with animals in heaven. It was an essay he felt Bubba would enjoy. But first he had to keep a promise. He told a young girl named Emily he would drop by to pray with her as she was fighting juvenile cancer. She was only a few years younger than Debi and was already facing a major life problem. On top of that she was depressed. It was a tough place for a nine-year-old to be in.

The house was very quiet as they knocked on the front door. The mother answered and looked very tired. She didn't even notice Bubba peeking from the pastor's coat.

"How are you doing, Vera?" he asked the mother.

"I'm OK, pastor. I just can't seem to bring any happiness to Emily. It's been a long journey, and though they say she is getting better, she doesn't see it."

"Well, let me talk to her and see what I can do."

After a short prayer, they walked down a hallway to Emily's dim bedroom. She was in bed and she brightened just a little bit when the pastor entered her room.

"I didn't think you'd come, pastor," and her facial expression fell again.

"Oh, Emily, I'll come whenever you want me to." He then led a beautiful prayer and ended saying after the amen, "By the way, I brought a friend of mine today."

"Where are they?" both Emily and her mother asked. Are they out in the car?" mother asked.

"No, no. I have him right here." Without letting Bubba know this was going to happen, he reached to his pocket and placed Bubba on Emily's lap.

"Oh, how cute," she said and began to pet Bubba softly. She was smiling.

"I can't leave him here because he belongs to Debi. You know her from church. She let me have him for a day so he could visit you specially. He's an amazing gerbil. His name is Bubba. If you ask him a question, he will nod his head yes or shake it no to answer you. Try him."

Bubba was at a loss. *What should I do? If I do this my gift will be revealed.* Suddenly he was overwhelmed that conversing was the right thing now. He'd do it.

Emily looked Bubba right in the eye. "Bubba, would you kiss me?"

He nodded yes and climbed up the bedclothes to kiss her on her cheek. When he did, she smiled a great big smile and he moved back to her lap.

Emily watched him carefully and spoke again, "Bubba, this is important. Can you really understand what I'm saying?

Yes, he nodded.

"Would you be my friend, too?

Yes, he nodded again and gave her a great double paw pump. As he did that, he was almost ready to cry as the question of what he should do with his life became clearer. *What a pleasant shock*, he thought. *I wonder where all this feeling of fulfillment is coming from?"*

Emily pet Bubba softly. "Do you know what cancer is?"

Yes.

"I have it." There was a pause. "Am I really getting better like my mom says?"

Bubba did another enthusiastic paw pump, ran in a couple of circles, did a summersault, and rose nodding yes vigorously. Then he added one more paw pump, and Emily laughed along with mom and the pastor. Emily took it as good news and smiled broadly.

Later, as they were leaving, Pastor promised to return again with Bubba and Emily's mom looked very pleased. "Thank you, Bubba. Be sure to come back. That's the first time Emily has smiled in months."

He waved to her from his high pocket. He hadn't felt this good in months either.

CHAPTER FIVE

A Therapy Gerbil

Bubba wanted to be sure he was right telling Emily she was getting better. As they drove to another home, Bubba and Pastor discussed what had happened. They decided together he did the right thing. Pastor assured him Emily's smile proved Bubba was on the right path. Of course, Bubba felt that way; he only needed Pastor's support.

For Bubba a life change occurred on Emily's bed; he felt it. Service to others made clear sense to him. He would never run away again; he'd give up lazing away in his habitat; he felt he needed to do more than be a friend to Debi, though that was a fine thing. Today the realization of what he needed to do became clear. Simply being a gerbil would never be enough again, and being a star for Father would never happen.

Pastor pulled into another drive way near Moorpark College. The townhome was similar to the home Debi lived in and was well kept. In fact, it was the house next to Debi's.

"Bubba, I know you expected me to drop you off at home so you could tell Debi about your new direction in life, but I pulled in here to take you in to meet a young man called Little Jack. Is that OK?"

Bubba nodded slowly.

"I needed to tell you about him though. He used to play in the street with Debi and the other neighbor kids. This was even before you went on your adventure.

"One day, while they were playing street soccer with a soft Nerf ball, Jack chased the ball under a car; he grabbed it and ran back into the street not noticing the other kids had moved aside for a car. He was hit by the car and went to the hospital in really bad condition. Whatever happened to him, he healed up pretty well but he never grew beyond his seven-year-old size and he can't walk. His mom schools him at home, and Jack doesn't go anywhere with the neighbor kids anymore. Debi tried for a year or so to get him interested in living again, be he became so depressed he won't do anything with anyone anymore.

"I've been visiting him twice a week for a long time now. I want you to see if you can perk him up. But I want to warn you, it's a very sad home."

Bubba looked at Pastor and nodded just a little. He was ready to meet Jack.

Pastor knocked on the door. A well-dressed mom answered and smiled at Pastor. "Jack is up and watching TV on his laptop. He may not even want to talk to you. I'm sorry."

"It's not a problem. I'm glad to be here."

They walked down the hallway and found Jack up and playing a game on his laptop. He was concentrating and barely acknowledged Pastor's presence.

"It's the only thing he enjoys, playing games. I'll leave you two alone," and Jack's mom left the room.

Bubba peeked over the edge of Pastor's pocket.

"Hi, Jack," Pastor said. "I came by with a friend today. You wanna meet him?"

Since no one seemed to be with the pastor, that caught Jack's attention. He shut his game down "Where is your friend? Still out there with mom?"

Pastor reached up and dropped Bubba gently onto the arm of Jack's chair. "Here he is. His name is Bubba."

"Isn't that Debi's old gerbil? He ran away and came back after several months, right"?

"Yes, Jack, but he has something he wants to say."

"What!? What do you mean he has something to say. Does he talk?"

"Sort of, Jack. Put your laptop in front of him and let's see."

Jack was slow to do so because he had to rearrange himself and his bedcovers before he could set Bubba up, but once that was done Bubba stepped onto the key board.

He typed, "Hi, Jack. I'm Bubba, yes Debi's old gerbil, and I'd like to get to know you better. Afterall, I live next door."

Jack looked at Pastor. "What's going on here, pastor? What's the trick?"

"No trick. He somehow learned to think and write like a human. Try him again."

After a few questions Jack became convinced Bubba was the real deal. "Do you play games?" Jack asked.

"I love word games like *Words with Friends*. The war games and car theft games are too difficult for me to play, but I can type in words easily. And I like to have time to think about answers. Maybe I am getting old. Is that OK?"

"Sure. Can you use the pastor's laptop? I'll play you a game."

After the two became involved in the word game, Pastor went next door to update Debi on what was happening. Then he talked with Father about it.

"Look, pastor," Father said, "I'm not a bad guy. Debi's gerbil is fine doing what he is doing. I won't run off with him to some TV producer, but what he is doing will be heard about. No doubt about that. I'll be sure to step in and help Debi and Bubba be stars at being, what did you call it?"

"A service animal. I called him a service animal or a therapy gerbil. It's hard to say what he is. But you are right, he will become famous sooner than later. We can't change that, but we can control how it takes place. Debi and Bubba will need help from you."

"I know that, and I will give it to them. Bubba's a free of charge helper to those who need him. That's totally fine with me. I still don't pretend to understand what's going on here."

"I can only speak from my position as a pastor. I've seen God do some amazing things, but this one even surprised me. I need to bring you the essay in my office talking about animals in Heaven. I don't doubt for a second that He's behind all this, and we need to keep working for Him."

They hadn't noticed, but earlier Debi slipped out and went next door. She watched Jack and Bubba playing *Words with Friends* and realized Jack would come out of his shell with Bubba's help, and she and Bubba would live happily ever after.

Printed in the United States
By Bookmasters